WHAT BECAME OF A WORLD THAT WAS

PERFECTLY
SQUARE

A FANTASY FABLE FOR ALL AGES

Dolly
Haik-Adams
Berthelot

diversity

change

creativity

teamwork

PERFECTLY SQUARE

Copyright © 1994, 2017, Dolly Berthelot

ISBN: 978-1-63199-336-7
LCCN: 2017943425

Energion Publications
P. O. Box 841
Gonzalez, FL 32560
2017

► *ACKNOWLEDGMENTS*

Helpmates are as varied as the shapes in this book.

For motivating, facilitating, and publishing new improved color versions of *PERFECTLY SQUARE*, I thank Energion Publications head Henry Neufeld, a long-time fan and friend who shares my commitment to fostering Unity Within Diversity. The new electronic and paperback versions relied on his wisdom, expertise, and devotion. Though my core story and art designs are intact, we added color, a fresh kaleidoscopic image, larger format, and fun details. This edition also includes extensive questions to provoke thought and discussion. Henry's technical mastery and endless patience were paramount as we collaborated to achieve my artistic vision. As in this fable, together we accomplished what neither of us could have done alone.

In the 1994 edition, Scott Miller did the main computer work, duplicating my designs. Other technical assistance then came from Laura White, Isaac Salpeter, and Bill Monk.

Several bookstores offered valuable feedback and later supportive distribution. Books-A-Million was then a primary book-signing venue throughout the South.

I appreciate the early insights and accolades of authors such as Fred Winkowski and of Nobel Peace Prize Winner Betty Williams, and numerous subsequent readers whose support and enthusiasm for *PERFECTLY SQUARE* spurred related creative ideas as well as eventually motivating this edition. Reader responses inspired me to develop SELFSHAPES™/

RELATIONSHAPES™ workshops and even theatrical productions, with more possibly on the horizon.

Unitarian Universalist Church of Pensacola (originally Pensacola UU Fellowship) has been a supportive venue for productions. Liz Brown, now Rev. Liz Brown, directed the first, with Jack Brookings and Maureen Henry doing duet reading. Janine Shoemaker directed the second, with Bill Whalen and the author doing duet reading. My later script evolved into an unusual musical, in which marvelous improvisational musicians bought each shape character to life. Thanks to these and other co-creators.

I'm grateful my late parents (Elaine Haik Adams and Malcolm Fielding Adams) encouraged us to be our own best selves. My five younger sisters and one brother and their families keep making the way more fun. My now late-husband Ron was both a rock of stability and a cushion of love. Our precious son Destin has nourished my inner child, challenged my assumptions, and sustained me with enduring love.

Students and clients never fail to teach me: late 1960s Oak Ridge High School (ETN) journalism, black studies, and English; early 1980s Loyola of the South journalism and communication; various college classes, plus, across the decades, numerous adults in communication, diversity, and teambuilding seminars in Pensacola and around the U.S.

Acquaintances, family, and friends powerfully shape our lives and empower us to live uniquely and fully. I cherish every kind thought, word, and deed.

PERFECTLY SQUARE is dedicated

to all who value the variety

of our ever-changing world

and appreciate the interdependence

that makes us one.

▶ Introduction

This wacky, intriguing story emerged from a twilight sleep "vision," in that magic time before, during, and after waking. The imagery came, like a gift from the "right brain," illustrating issues of human diversity, change, conflict, teamwork, and creativity which were, and have long been, among my personal and professional obsessions. Thereafter, for five years my "left brain" held the work hostage, in perpetual revision and put aside for more prosaic matters.

Like much in my life, this quirky tale does not seem to fit existing molds. Is *PERFECTLY SQUARE* for adults or children? Is its purpose to teach, to inspire, or "merely" to delight? I hope, any and all of these. Different readers will bring their own needs, inclinations, and perspectives to this work, which I call, for lack of a better label, a fantasy fable.

Above all, enjoy.

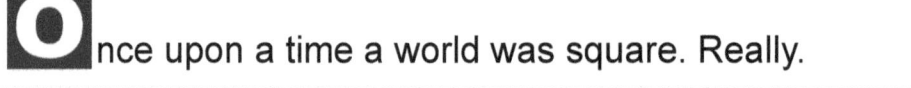

Once upon a time a world was square. Really.

Everything on it—including all living creatures—was square, perfectly square. In fact, everything was made up of two-inch squares that multiplied (by two of course) to reproduce. Methodically. They joined together to form larger objects, even older square creatures, all easily divisible by two. Birthdays meant add a year and add a square!

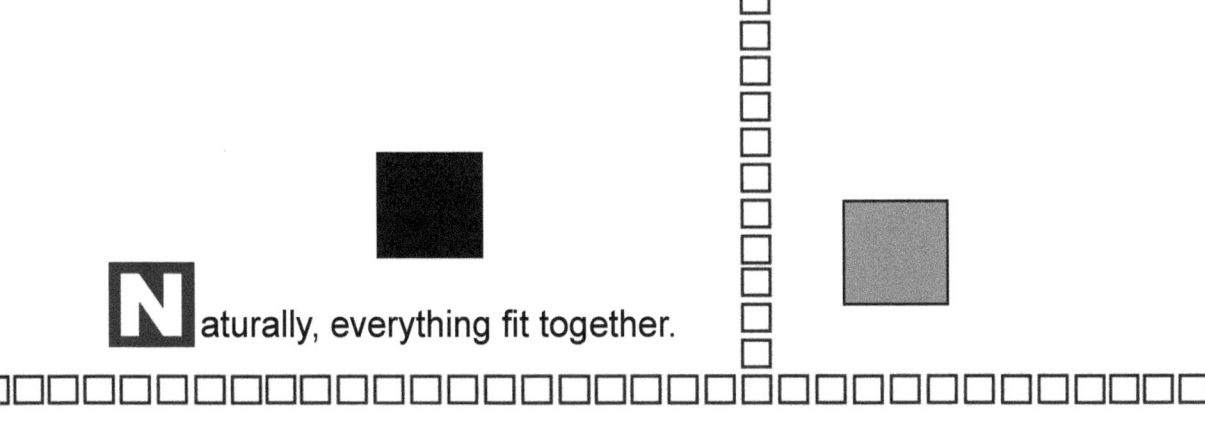

aturally, everything fit together.

Everyone knew just what to expect, and they did

expect just that: absolute, measurable, predictable

perfection. Which everyone recognized, of course,

and agreed upon. Without question.

Squareland had no conflict.

Squareness certainly had benefits. Clothes, cars, and characters were interchangeable. Mass production was very mass, therefore very cheap, so living costs were low. Uniformity tended to prevent competitiveness. Why would anyone care to "keep up with the Joneses," when everything, and everyone, was so very much the same? Life was simple. Easy.

Roads were impeccably straight and simple to follow, yards were quick to mow, marching units didn't miss a beat. High rises were safely built to the clouds without toppling. Some connected to each other by an enclosed bridge, a sky mall, the ultimate closed-air living, shopping, working, playing center. "Getting there" was soooo easy. Who could imagine it any other way?

Young squares enjoyed playing outside together. Children and nature were the least predictable elements in that predictable world. They liked to swing high on square swings, climb across square-bars, and scamper neatly through their made-to-order square tunnel. Some shared cosmically-popular kids' games like Hide and Seek, Follow the Leader, and the game that changed everything—

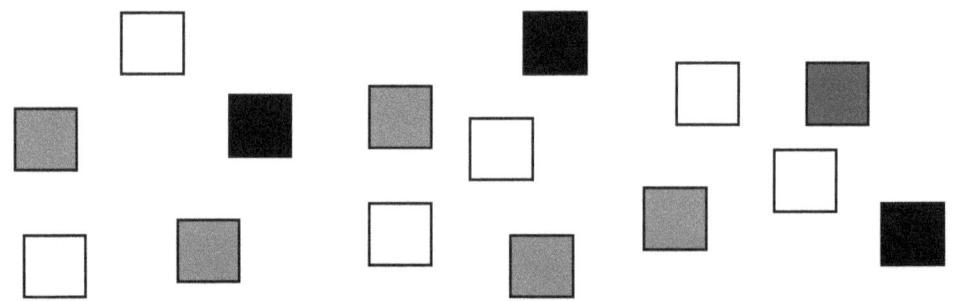

Red Rover Red Rover, Send ??? Right Over.

One team lined up (perfectly straight), joined together

and (in the singsong of universal childhood) called

a member of the opposite team. "Red Rover, Red

Rover send DB4688x right over." DB4688x had

to run over and break through. The line held tight,

braced for action. And action they got!

Now, the running square was a cheerful little cut-up, a shade brighter (but clumsier) than most. The child was racing into the line of squares—then someone unexpectedly called out: "Hey, DB!"

The sharp young square crashed into the living barrier, turned abruptly, and sliced EA822k in two! Whoops!!

No one was hurt, since Squareland creatures can heal and reproduce themselves, but the sliced one was certainly changed. There stood two stunned rectangles!

(A concept yet to be identified and named, since it was outside Squareland's known reality, but rectangles even so.) The amazed group saw their friend as two very funny, very messed up squares. And for a while, that's how they saw themselves. All the perfect squares laughed hysterically at the weird transformation.

Luckily, the rectangles had a sense of humor and simply joined the fun. One jostled a friend to the ground and pinned one corner to its opposite.

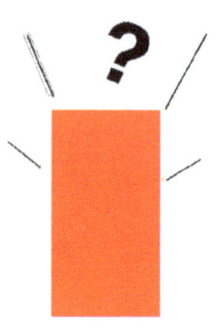

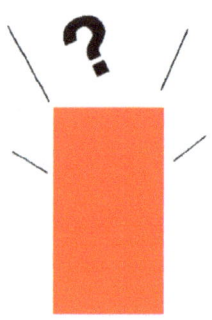

POP! The

square snapped and
each separate
Both were
then

formed 2 triangles
but equal,
stunned,
giddy.

The spirit was contagious!

Triangles

poked squares in the center

and blew them up like balloons,

creating the Square World's very first circles.

Especially adventuresome, one circle drifted

up and off, instantly. To make the other circle

stay put, the quick thinking new rectangle

instantly sat on him. The perfect

roundness scrunched ever-so-

slightly into an ellipse—

a circle with an identity crisis!

While the ellipse sulked a bit over being forced too hastily beyond his circle phase, most loved the exciting new shapes. So they created more sizes and shapes to join the fun. And what fun it was!

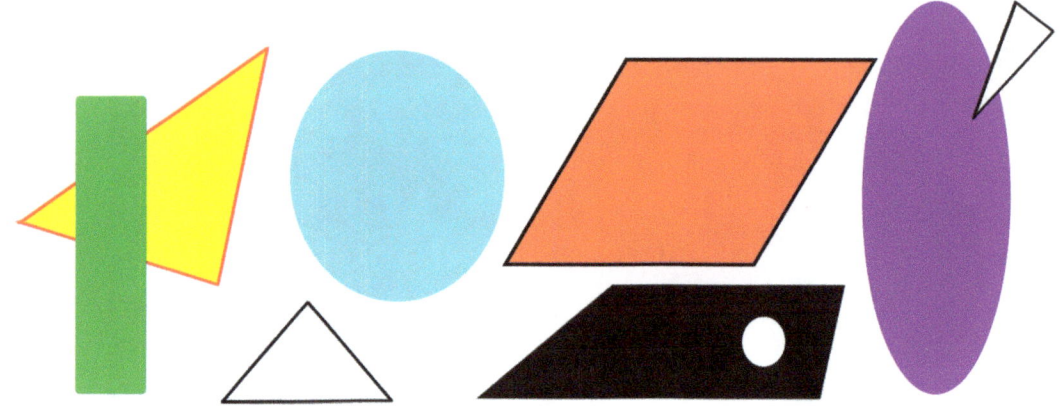

Creativity erupted like spontaneous combustion. Instinctively, the children built on their differences. Triangles became sailboats and church steeples or pointy noses on which fantastic new balls could bounce.

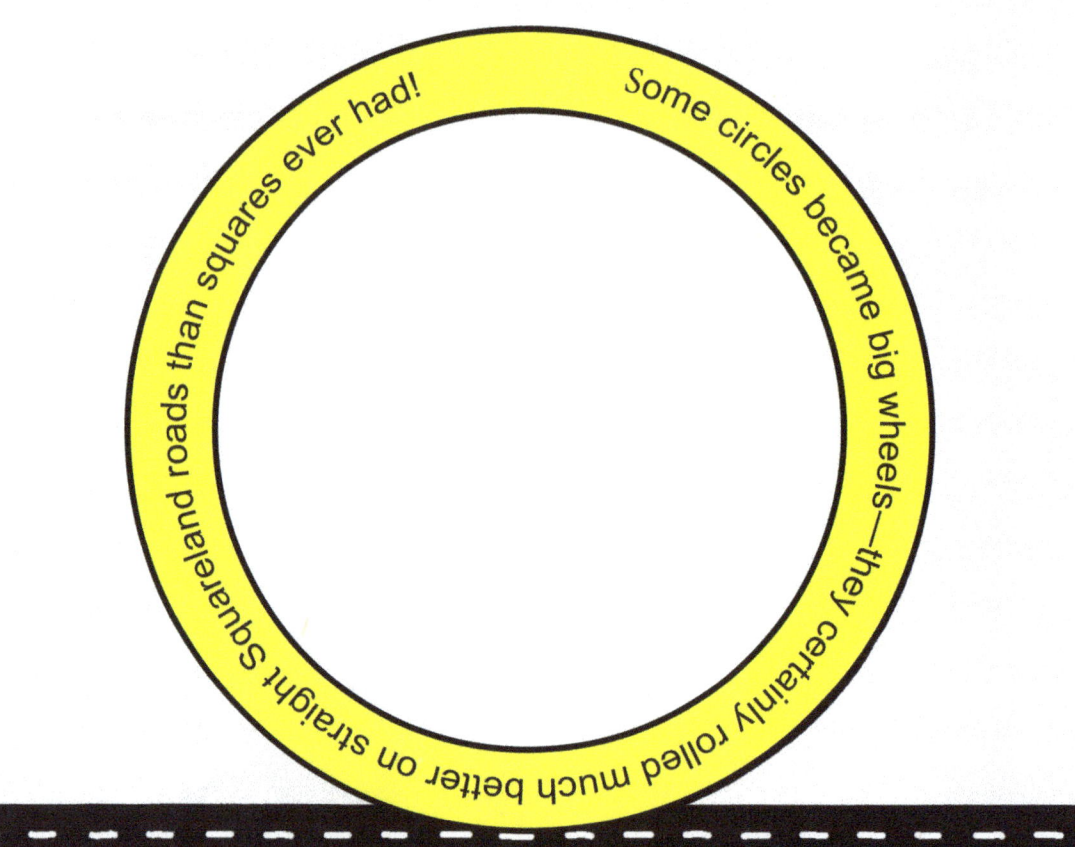

Some circles became big wheels—they certainly rolled much better on straight Squareland roads than squares ever had!

22

Eventually, mere circumstance changed other squares. Unusually hearty eaters grew into fat trapezoids.

A few squares, swept by a hurricane, became slanted parallelograms. They seemed always on the move....

ome circles were clipped and filed into fancy

polygons—hexagons and octagons

and their stranger kin.

A few very talented "gons" and triangles

collaborated to become stars,

REAL STARS !

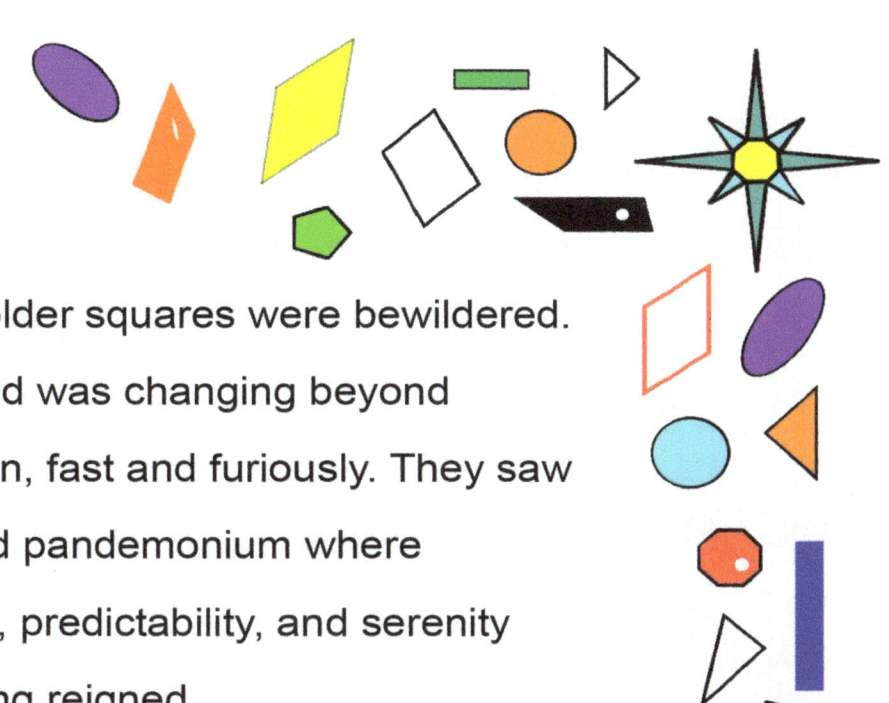

Most older squares were bewildered. Their world was changing beyond recognition, fast and furiously. They saw chaos and pandemonium where uniformity, predictability, and serenity had so long reigned.

Frantic efforts failed to keep the little squares perfect squares, as did all attempts to rehabilitate those who had forever altered their basic squareness.

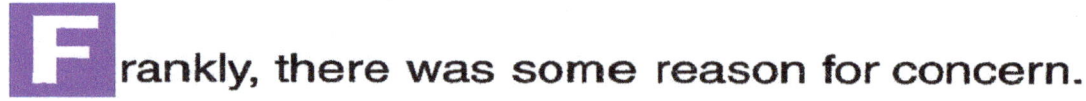

Frankly, there was some reason for concern.

No one could predict

what would happen next,

much less where or when.

Planning was tougher.

When kids forgot themselves and raced through the square tunnel, they would get stuck and have to be pried loose. Ouch!

Neither clothes nor concepts

nor characters were interchangeable.

Now, little could be done unthinkingly. Buying was a nightmare of complexity and over choice. To satisfy the rapidly changing markets, products were raced out too hastily, and at increasingly exorbitant costs.

Neither schools nor jobs could keep pace with the changing personnel pool, and working with such strange creatures wasn't always easy.

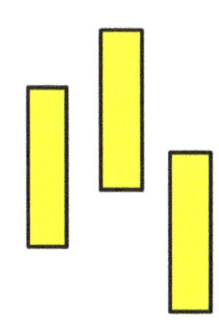

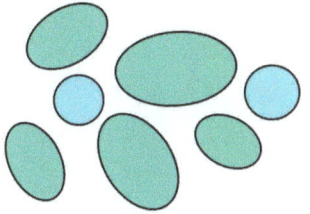

As various shapes reached adolescence, they formed the inevitable cliques.

The conflict-free

Violence sometimes broke out.

Many were afraid.

They yearned for the old order.

Who could blame them?

world was shattered.

Diversity was clearly a challenge.

Change supplanted comfort.

Tensions mounted between groups.

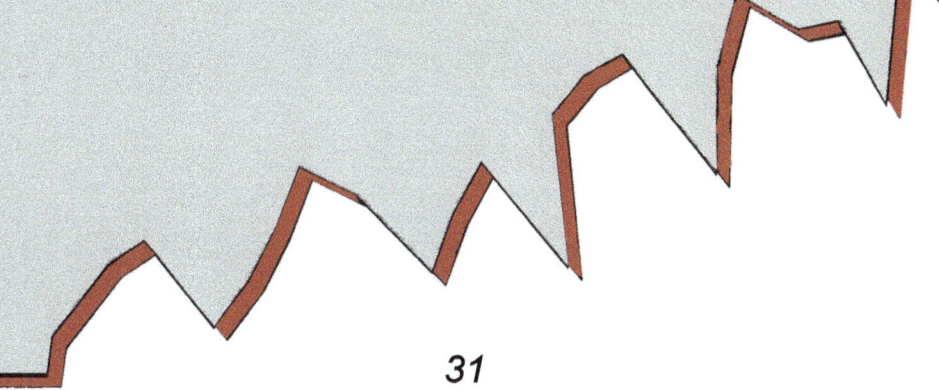

Being

remarkably sharp, triangles

could be dangerous. They were also

on the cutting edge, making interesting new

shapes. Triangles became innovators, mavericks, surprise

assets in this rapidly changing world. Triangles

could pierce false assumptions, cut

red tape—and point the way

like no one

else.

Circles were philosophical, conjuring abstract ideals of all-embracing, never-ending love, inter-connectedness, infinitude, and pi. True, they were not understood by many, but criticism rolled easily off their backs.

Flighty circles often drifted off (in their imagination and in geographic reality), to be respected, generations later, as masters...

...especially by erudite young

parallelograms (who tended to

become teachers and scholars with

a fondness for big words).

Many parallelograms changed lives and were cherished forever. The best heeded a wise circle's urge: "Follow your bliss," and produced some real gems.

In contrast, rectangles were great building

blocks and balancing beams, skilled workers

you

could

count on.

Stable.

Strong.

Almost

square.

Eventually, adventuresome squares of all ages experimented with different shapes, but most recognized some long-ignored advantages of squareness, even as they learned the value of variation. Squares formed a solid, dependable foundation. In fact, they were more appreciated than ever, as their unique (and essential) sturdiness and predictability became less taken for granted.

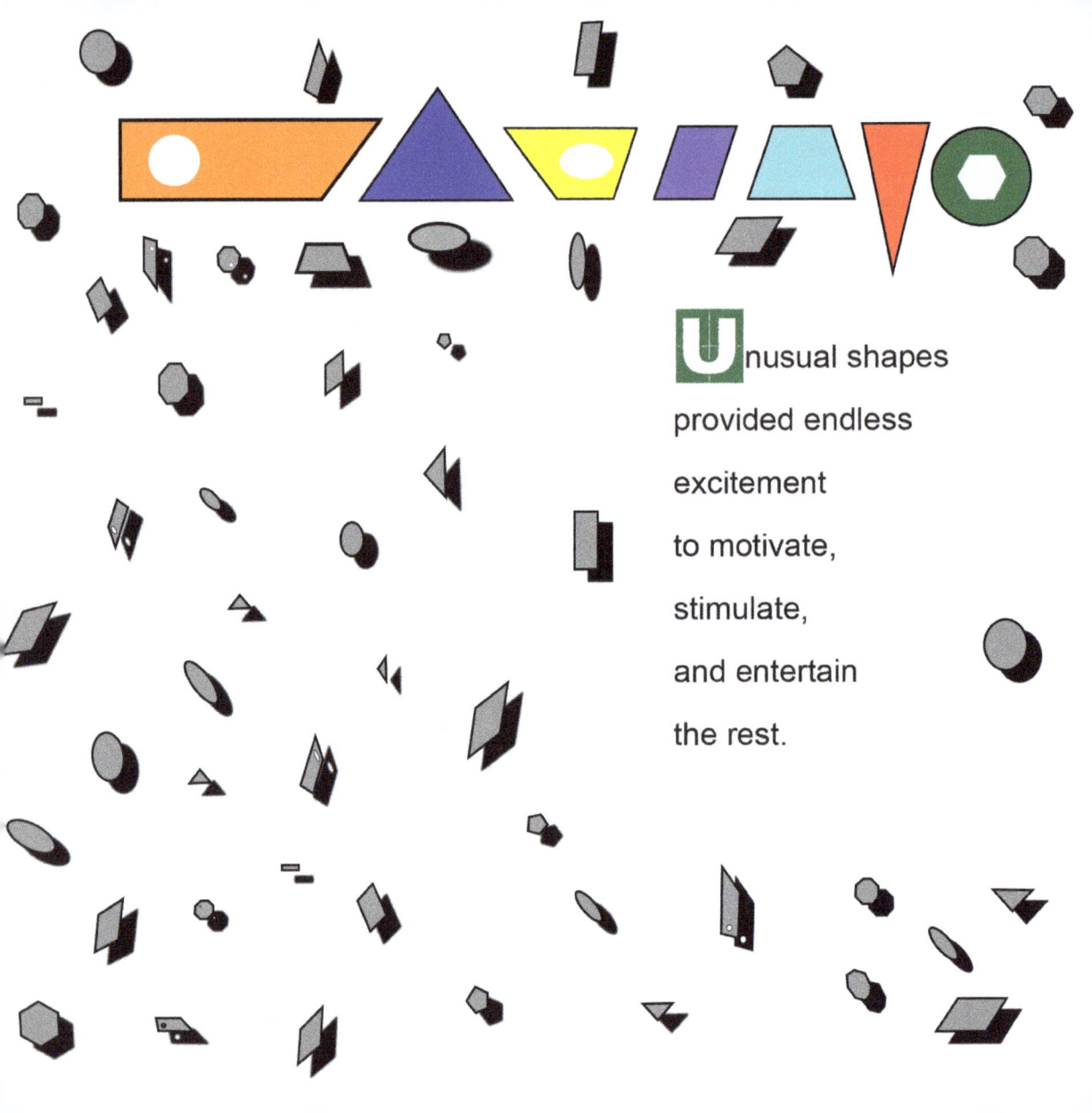

Unusual shapes
provided endless
excitement
to motivate,
stimulate,
and entertain
the rest.

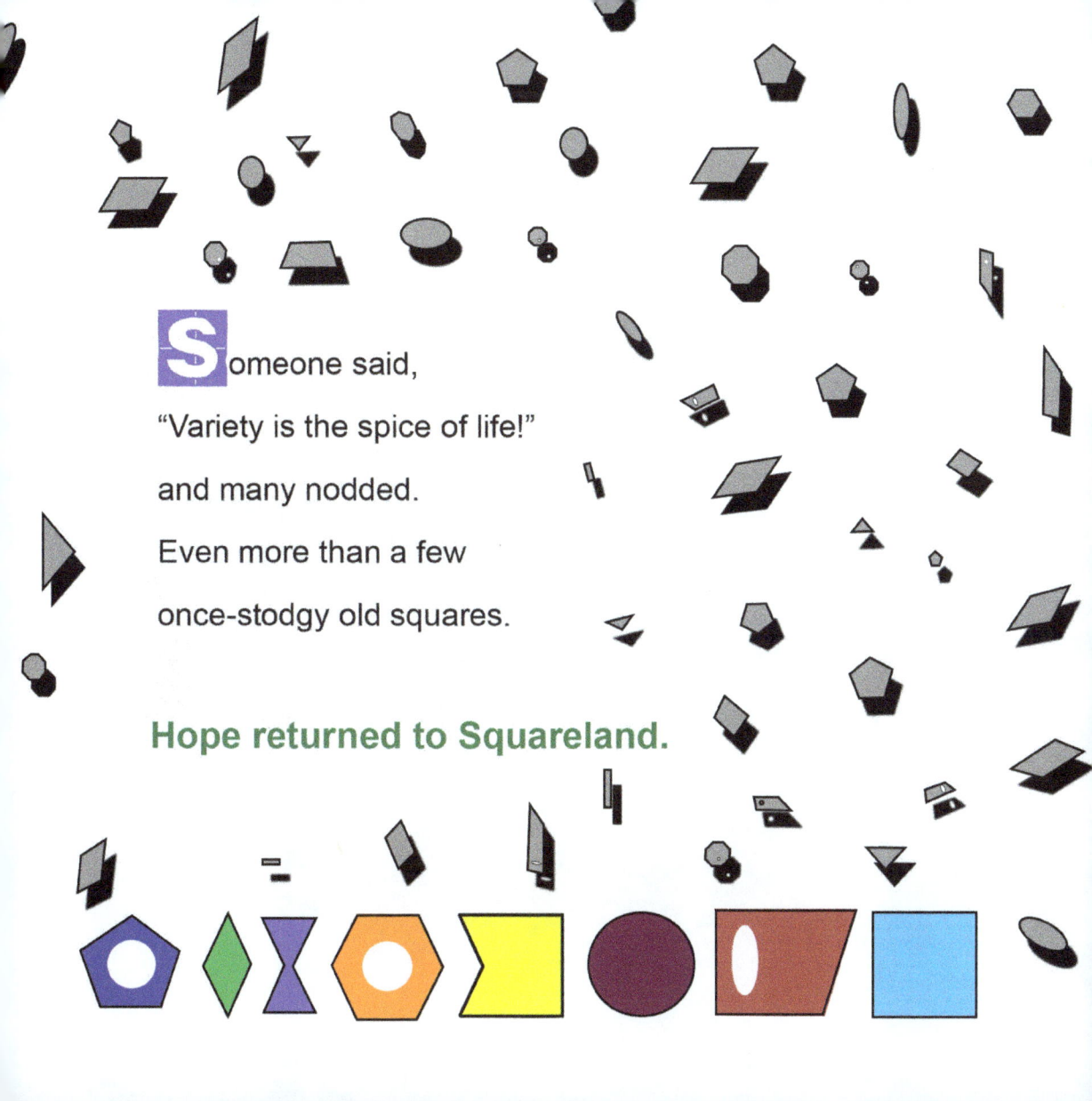

Someone said,

"Variety is the spice of life!"

and many nodded.

Even more than a few

once-stodgy old squares.

Hope returned to Squareland.

Everyone tried a little harder
to make relationships a little softer.

ltimately,

tensions were replaced by tolerance,

finally, even genuine appreciation for all.

Various shapes learned to accept

and cherish themselves AND each other.

They now recognized how each

weird and wonderful variation

contributed—uniquely—to the whole.

Reality showed that the principles of effective design are as relevant to life as to any art. Contrast, variety, balance, harmony.

CONTRAST • VARIETY • BALANCE • HARMONY

Omit any element and the design fails.

With this wisdom in action, the creatures achieved far more than they ever could have as either clones or adversaries.

Eventually, they learned to work together for the common good.

Teamwork didn't always come easy, mind you, for anyone. All those differences! There were frustrations, challenges, even a few bruises along the way, but they surely enjoyed playing around with fresh options....

Having less to unlearn and a natural drive to learn more, children continued to set the pace, often serendipitously.

One play group happened to have samples of many diverse shapes and sizes.

They had been building together for some time by then, and had established real teamwork.

As they frolicked in the yard together

one sunny afternoon,

an astounding thing occurred.

It started without plan or fanfare.

Two solid squares stood beside each other

a few feet apart.

Seizing the moment,

two slim rectangles

quickly shimmied over

and stacked on top of each square.

It was party time!

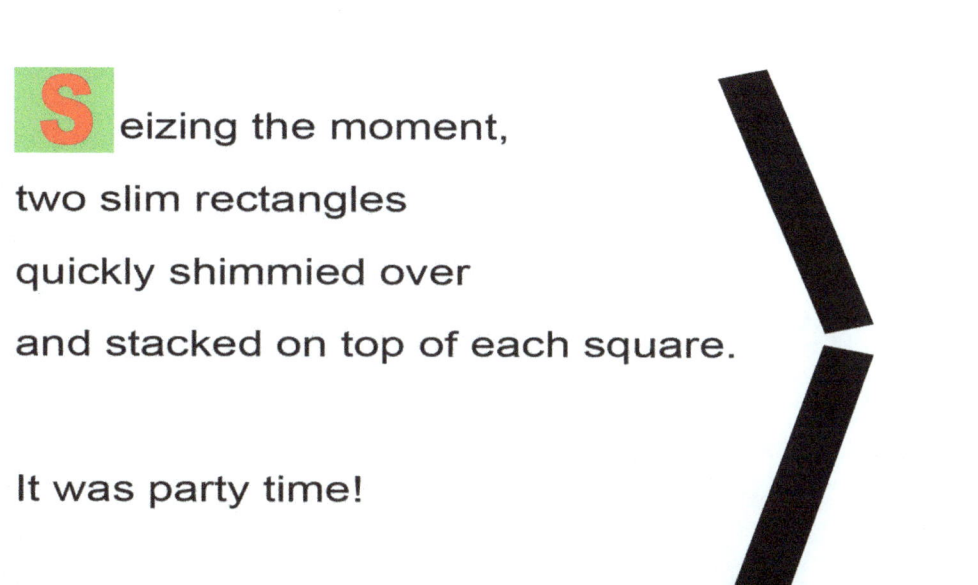

A big ellipse teetered on top of all that.

Flailing triangles attached to each side.

Other shapes were improvising music and

applauding wildly.

One circle plopped on top wearing a jaunty trapezoid hat decorated by gentle ellipses. A very small and talkative hexagon climbed onto the lower part of the circle. A smaller ellipse split and carried dark balls up to the top half of the circle.
I do believe one winked.

By playing and working
together, using the distinctions
of each, the diverse shapes
formed a primitive prototype
of a future being.

Their unique creation
combined the very best
of each into the very best of all.
Delight infused a new spirit
with faint traces of
a growing heart.

Someday,

such new beings

would be called human.

And they would be

wonderfully far

from perfectly square.

How does *PERFECTLY SQUARE* apply to challenges and opportunities in...

▲ your life?

◯ your relationships?

◇ your work—and play?

▽ your class or school?

▮ your church, temple, or mosque?

● your other organizations?

▢ your community?

⬠ your nation?

▶ your world?

I encourage readers and users of PERFECTLY SQUARE, alone and in groups, to use these questions to stimulate perceptions, ideas, interactions, and creativity. Adapt questions for various ages, purposes and needs. Add your own as they come to you. Play with possibilities.

Suggestion: Jotting down your responses may also be useful. Reread, reconsider yearly.

And please, share your thoughts, ideas, and uses of PERFECTLY SQUARE with me. I'll be glad to hear from you, and to help you in any way I can.

--Dr. Dolly Berthelot, drdollyb@gmail.com, drdollyb.com/diversity

☐ **What did you especially *ENJOY* about this little book?**

☐ **List various human-related messages you see reflected in this story.**

☐ **How does the simple art support and enhance the verbal content?**

☐ **What message or theme spoke most significantly to you? Why?**

☐ **Do the descriptions of various shapes' personalities make sense to you?**

☐ **How have you felt bullied, mistreated, or shunned for being "different"?**

☐ **How can you imagine the book being used to consider issues in your own family, school, organization, workplace, etc.?**

☐ **How might the story and characters come to life beyond this book?**

Suggestion: Return to overview questions after exploring the rest.

☐ **Look around your room and spot various geometric shapes. What would be missing if there were less variety? Why would we want human sameness?**

☐ **Considering descriptions in *PERFECTLY SQUARE* and your own observations, what shape or shapes are you most like?**

☐ **What potentially positive and negative qualities do you perceive in the various shapes as related to human traits or tendencies?**

☐ **What shapes typify some important people in your life?**

☐ **List all the existing forms of human diversity you can think of.**

☐ **List some real, practical advantages of homogeneity or sameness.**

☐ **List some real, practical advantages of heterogeneity or diversity.**

☐ **List some forms of human diversity now in your life. Which challenge you?**

- [ ] **What consistency or routines do you especially like or feel you need?**

- [ ] **What tough changes have you confronted?**

- [ ] **What tough changes do you now face?**

- [ ] **Change often means both loss and gain. How have you gained or can you perhaps gain from loss?**

- [ ] **What are your natural reactions and your typical approaches to change?**

- [ ] **What change response could possibly better serve you—or serve others?**

- [ ] **What would you especially like to change right now? Why?**

- [ ] **What blocks a change or changes you think might be beneficial?**

- [ ] **Who might help that change happen? How can you encourage that help?**

☐ Note how various examples of change and creativity occur in this fable. How might those examples relate to real life?

☐ Play and humor spur creativity. Have you ever created something worthwhile—tangible or "just an idea"—while playing around?

☐ How can playfulness and humor become more powerfully present or active in your life?

☐ Share an idea, innovation, or creation you are proud of. How did it occur?

☐ In your fantasies, what would you like to try to become, build, or create? Don't imprison possibilities.

☐ Conflict is not always bad. How can conflict be used beneficially, creatively? What have you ever learned from a particular conflict?

☐ Contrast, Variety, Balance, Harmony. How might these principles of effective design (p. 42) be useful in your relationships? In your life?

☐ For fun, put together some basic geometric shapes to draw something, as done in this book.

☐ What advantages do you see in having people who are different from you work with you on some goal or project?

☐ Of the 8 shape characters described in *PERFECTLY SQUARE*, with which are you most likely to have difficulty? Why?

☐ How can those shapes that may challenge you also benefit you?

☐ How can people who disagree achieve something valuable—more valuable—together? Share any relevant experiences.

☐ Who or what might help you reach a goal? How could that happen?

☐ Who could you help reach a goal? How could that happen?

☐ What "common good" should you be working toward? Are you? How committed are you? Who joins you?

Suggestions: A self-administered SELFSHAPES™ survey and Dr. Dolly workshops such as SELFSHAPES™ and RELATIONSHAPES™ expand on the ideas suggested in the book and in these questions. For more info see http://drdollyb.com/ps.

Dolly Haik-Adams Berthelot tends to "shape shift" between—and integrate—multiple worlds. She has taught public school, college and university levels (Loyola University of the South and others) and myriad adult learners; edited daily and weekly newspapers and created a Smoky Mountains anthology; published articles and photos internationally; and dabbled in arts and antiques. Writing is a constant friend.

Dr. Dolly earned MS and EdD degrees from University of Tennessee (Communication/Journalism and Adult Curriculum and Instruction) and a BA in English from Southeastern Louisiana University.

She grew up in Bogalusa, LA. Being the eldest of seven, with Lebanese-American and German-American parents, taught her early about diversity. She has been learning ever since.

After years as a communication and human relations consultant and seminar leader for organizations large and small, Dr. Dolly now prepares to publish her own memoirs and quirky fiction while satisfying select clients' varied writing and communication needs. She continues providing a few individuals and organizations with her unique expertise, creative services, and occasionally workshops, such as innovative Mine Your Memories for Life Stories™, SELF-SHAPES™, and RELATIONSHAPES™, in which participants play with shapes to expand the perfectly human issues in *PERFECTLY SQUARE*.

Besides writing, editing, teaching, and coaching, the author relishes living by the water in lovely, historic Pensacola, FL, while enjoying people, art, theater, music, lectures, quality films, reading, beauty, and travel, as she can.

You may learn more at drdollyb.com and mineyourmemories1.com.

PERFECTLY SQUARE and helpful related products are available from Energion Direct where you can order online and pay by credit card or check.

Dealer/Bulk Inquiries
Call: 850-525-3916
E-mail: pubs@energion.com
Web: http://energion.com

- **NEW Color Paperback Edition,** available July. 2017, $12.99 (Quantity discounts available)
- **NEW Color e-book edition,** available for Kindle and ePub readers (iBooks, Google Play, and others). Check http://drdollyb.com/ps for current ebook purchasing links.
- **Paperback B&W First Edition**, while supplies last, $5.00 (Special Sale)

STIMULATING PS QUESTIONS are included in new color editions. First edition buyers may order optional separate 20 questions fold over. $1.75 only with classic B&W edition order.

PERFECTLY SQUARE - Related Products

- **What Shape Are You In?** Short self-analysis inventory links your behavioral traits to 8 universal geometric shapes. Novel human types system, useful for self development and for teambuilding. $5.
- **SELFSHAPES™ and RELATIONSHAPES™ Workshops** offer fresh angles on yourself and others. Two 3-hour modules, innovative right- and left-brain activities. 8.5" x 11" booklet, approximately 12 pages per module. Ordered and mailed together, $15.

► **ANOTHER UNIQUE DR. DOLLY PUBLICATION**
PIONEER SPIRIT 76, the (US) BicenTENNial Anthology of the Smoky Mountains Region. $14.00
Beautiful softcover book provides fascinating articles and gorgeous photos of Southern Appalachian history, culture, and nature. It is now a rare, limited edition collector's item.

Creative Communication

Dr Dolly Berthelot

◘ writer ◘ editor ◘ consultant ◘ coach

life stories--
mineyourmemories1.com

unity in diversity--
drdollyb.com

drdollyb@gmail.com

- Consulting, counseling
- Professional writing
- Dynamic workshops

- In-depth interviewing
- Polished editing
- Group facilitation

Go play!

With all kinds of people.

You never know

what you might discover—

or create...

www.ingramcontent.com/pod-product-compliance
Lightning Source LLC
Chambersburg PA
CBHW041133170626
46815CB00009B/351